THE FIRST WORLD WAR

At the beginning of the twentieth century, most countries in Europe had empires that stretched all over the world. These empires had aligned themselves into two major blocks. If one member of a block went to war, the others had to follow. The empires had also built huge armies and had developed large arsenals of weapons, which they were eager to use. Because of this situation, on June 28, 1914, when Archduke Franz Ferdinand, the heir to the throne of Austria-Hungary was assassinated, the First World War broke out.

Canada, while no longer a British colony, remained a close ally of Great Britain as did other countries in the Commonwealth. Canadian soldiers joined the British and their allies, France and Russia, almost immediately. Germany fought with Austria-Hungary. The United States did not come into the war until 1917, when it joined the British-French alliance.

Everyone thought the war would only last a few months, but they were wrong. Nearly ten million soldiers and thirteen million civilians died because of the war, which did not end until 1918. The whole twentieth century was shaped and affected by this event, which many people believe was a direct cause of World War Two.

To Fanny R.

Groundwood Books / Douglas & McIntyre
720 Bathurst Street, Suite 500, Toronto, Ontario M5S 2R4

Distributed in the USA by Publishers Group West
1700 Fourth Street, Berkeley, CA 94710

We acknowledge for their financial support of our publishing program the Canada Council for the Arts, the Ontario Arts Council and the Government of Canada through the Book Publishing Industry Development Program (BPIDP).

ONTARIO ARTS COUNCIL
CONSEIL DES ARTS DE L'ONTARIO

National Library of Canada Cataloguing in Publication Data
Debon, Nicolas
A brave soldier
ISBN 0-88899-481-8
1. Soldiers--Canada--Juvenile Fiction. 2. World War, 1939-1945--Juvenile fiction. I. Title.
PS8557.E2285B73 2002   jC813'.6   C2001-903207-2
PZ7.D339252Br 2002

Nicolas Debon's illustrations are done in Winsor and Newton acrylics, in a narrow range of colors, on Arches cold-pressed watercolor paper.
Book design by Michael Solomon
Printed and bound in China by Everbest Printing Co. Ltd.

A Brave Soldier

Nicolas Debon

A GROUNDWOOD BOOK

Douglas & McIntyre

TORONTO VANCOUVER BERKELEY

Frank was on his way home one evening in August when he heard a loud noise in the distance.

A few blocks ahead, he came upon a crowd of men shouting, waving flags and beating drums.

"War! War! Canada is at war!"

His older friend Michael was in the crowd.

"Frankie, come and join up!" he called. "Let's go whip the Germans. It'll be easy and we'll be home by Christmas."

Frank didn't know anything about the war, or about Germans. He enlisted in the army because he didn't want anyone to think he was a coward.

When it came time for the platoon to leave, the whole town gathered at the station. The band often interrupted the mayor's farewell speech. The blasts from the steam whistles made Frank jump.

His mother cried a little and waved her white handkerchief when the train left. But Michael's sweetheart blew kisses and ran along the tracks.

"Take care," called the fathers.

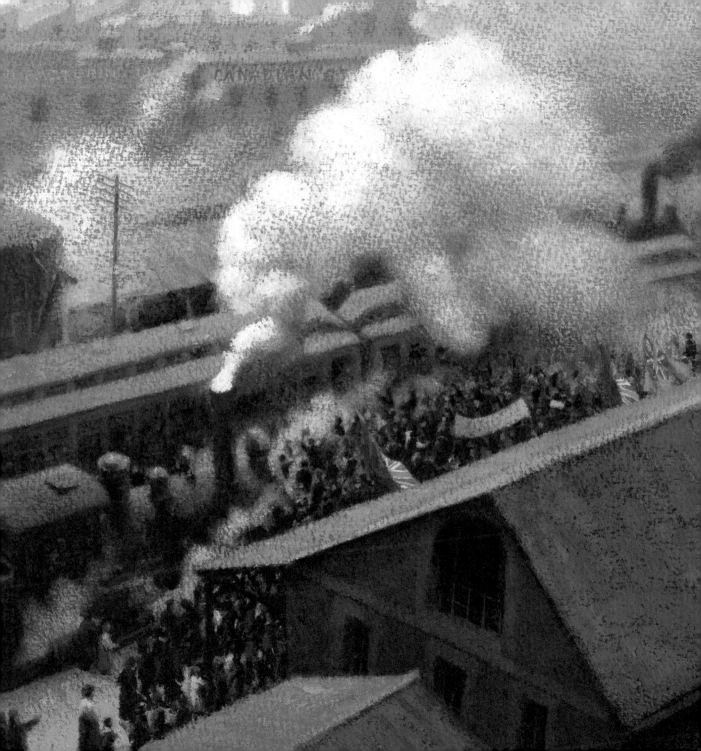

It was October by the time Frank and his platoon mates were ready to board the huge ship that would take them across the Atlantic Ocean to Europe. Every nook and cranny of the boat was piled with equipment. Guns, cases of ammunition, horses and food rations had to be stowed, and the men squeezed into any leftover spaces.

On deck, a group of soldiers formed around Michael. As always he was telling jokes and making fun of their commanders or scary Kaiser Wilhelm of Germany. Frank had to laugh, but inside he felt a little afraid.

Ten days later, the convoy reached England, where Frank spent the whole winter and rainy spring in a training camp. Frank was almost relieved when the order came to cross the English Channel for the battlefront.

When they reached France, the soldiers were packed into a long line of trucks, which drove slowly over muddy roads. Stopping and starting, it took forever before Frank and his companions were finally dropped off near a ruined town.

As the platoon marched in silence to the battlefront, the booming of artillery could be heard in the distance.

An endless column of horse-drawn wagons, ambulances and French soldiers — their blue uniforms covered in mud — was coming the other way.

"How is it up there?" asked Michael.

"It's terrible. It's like hell," replied a tall African soldier. "Where are you from?"

"Canada."

A scout guided them through a maze of deep ditches to the front line. The mud made everything dirty and slippery, but the worst was the terrible stench that filled the air.

Across an empty patch of ground called No Man's Land lay the German trenches, hidden behind a pile of tangled barbed wire. The scout told Frank that at night he would be able to hear the Germans talking, they were so close.

Slowly Frank became used to this new life. All the soldiers had to carry water and food rations, make repairs to the trenches and take turns keeping watch for enemy raids.

Whenever Frank had free time and he wasn't trying to snatch a few hours of sleep, he read, wrote letters to his parents and played cards. Michael loved talking about the baseball team back home, of which he'd been the captain. While he listened, Frank worked on getting rid of the lice that infested his clothes and hair and made him itch.

One afternoon, an officer came up.

"We have received orders from headquarters. We will attack tomorrow morning," he said. "Good luck, boys."

He tapped Frank on the shoulder and left.

In the middle of the night Frank heard heavy guns firing from behind him. The ground was shaking, and the sky was lit up behind enemy lines as though it were day.

For the first time, Frank thought about the Germans over there. He wondered if they also had homes and families waiting for them in Germany. This gave him a strange, disagreeable feeling.

The bombing stopped.

Frank and his platoon mates stood side by side on the fire step of the trench, shivering in the cold night. No one dared to say a word.

"Now!" shouted an officer, who had been looking at his watch.

Whistles blew. One by one, the soldiers climbed over the parapet and slowly moved out over No Man's Land toward the Germans.

They had just reached enemy lines when shells started bursting around them.

Frank saw the man next to him fall, shot by a machine gun. He was scared.

He shouted as loudly as he could but he couldn't hear his own voice over the deafening noise.

There was silence when Frank woke up. He had a terrible pain in his leg. He could not move, and he felt thirsty and cold. He looked around and saw that he was lying in a hole that had been made by a huge cannon shell.

Beside him, drowning in the mud as he was, lay soldiers whose faces he could not make out. He couldn't even tell if they were dead or alive.

After a moment, he heard voices speaking in German.

Two soldiers were walking toward him. Frank was terrified. He was sure they were coming to kill him. He tried to play dead, but one of the soldiers came closer.

"Kamerad, Kamerad, we mean no harm!" said the man in a soft voice. "We are prisoners of war helping to bring in the wounded."

The stretcher-bearers took him to a dressing station where dozens of soldiers were lying side by side. Some of the wounded were wearing German uniforms. Many men were missing arms or legs. One had a hole where his mouth used to be. Frank noticed that some men just lay shaking or whimpering over and over. But no matter where Frank turned he could not find Michael.

"Hmm...you have shrapnel in your leg. You'll be lucky to keep it," said a doctor. "I'm afraid the war is over for you, kid."

Frank was recovering when he learned on November 11, 1918, that the war had ended, four years after it had begun.

The last thing he did before taking the ship home to Canada was to visit the military cemetery where Michael was buried. Frank thought about his friend and about the young Germans whose voices he used to hear on the other side of No Man's Land. He wondered what had happened to them. The cold winter wind made him shiver.

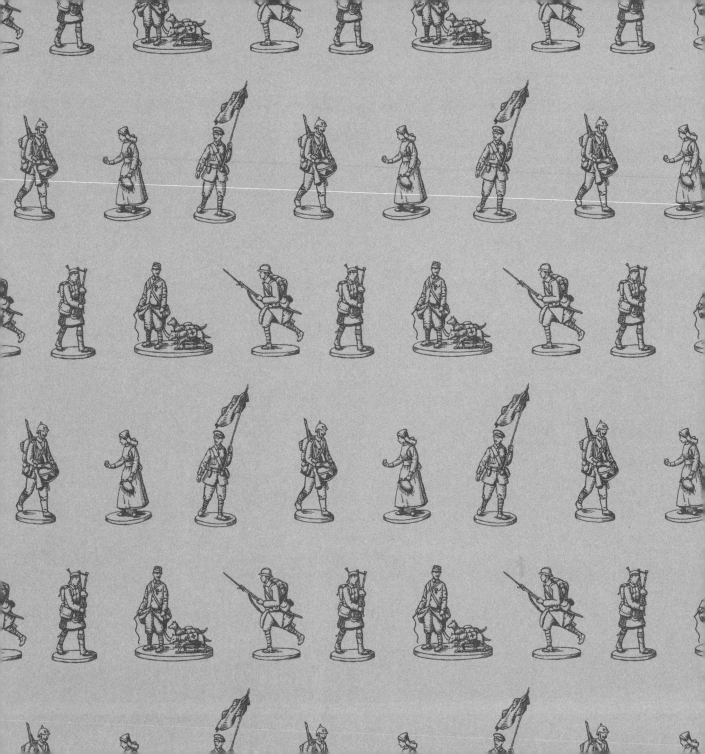